ADVENTURE TIME™

HOW TO
CATCH A PRINCESS

awesome words by Max Brallier

kick-butt illustrations by Shane L. Johnson

PSS!
PRICE STERN SLOAN
An Imprint of Penguin Group (USA) LLC

PRICE STERN SLOAN
Published by the Penguin Group
Penguin Group (USA) LLC, 375 Hudson Street, New York, New York 10014, USA

USA | Canada | UK | Ireland | Australia | New Zealand | India | South Africa | China

penguin.com
A Penguin Random House Company

Published in 2013 by Price Stern Sloan, a division of Penguin Young Readers Group, 345 Hudson Street, New York, New York 10014. PSS! is a registered trademark of Penguin Group (USA) LLC. Printed in the U.S.A.

ISBN 978-0-8431-7525-7   10 9 8 7 6 5 4 3 2 1

This isn't a diary! It's a guide!
A guide to catching princess ladies!
And it belongs to

_____

If anybody else touches it,
the Ice King will punch 'em in the boingloings.

Like I've been saying for years, princesses are the best and I want them all.

As you know from watching my television program, *Ice King Time*, I'm very smooth and suave. I'm an affection magnet. For me, catching princesses is supereasy. I'm just like, "Hey, Princess, want some love hugs?" and they start swooning.

But, what's that, you say? You want *me* to show *you* the tricks of the trade? How to mack on hotties?

Then let this book be your guide . . .

The Ice King is a filthy, filthy liar.

That's not the name of the show, Ice Jerk!

ICE KING WISDOM

To get you started, here are some awesome things I've said to make princesses want to cuddle:

I'll show you fun. Fun is my middle name.

I'm rockin' your worldview!

I just want to be loved!

I take artful black-and-white photographs of my penguins.

I try so hard to be a good husband to girls . . .

Write your own silky smooth love-liners below. If you can't think of anything icy cool to say, just jot down some of your favorite *Adventure Time* quotes.

_____

_____

_____

_____

_____

_____

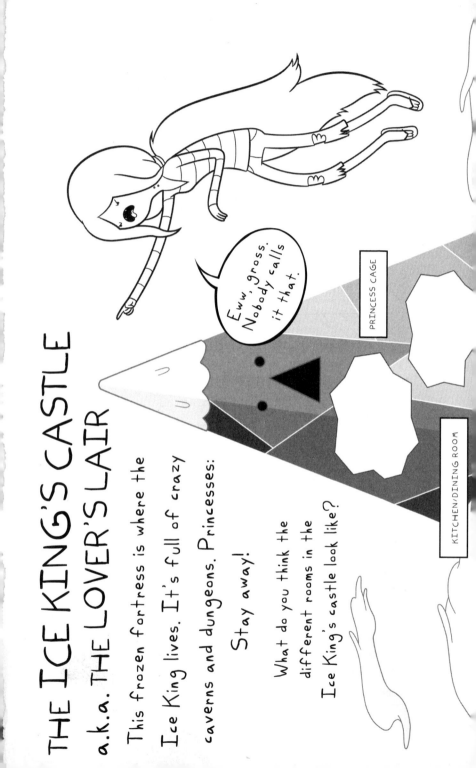

THE ICE KING'S CASTLE
a.k.a. THE LOVER'S LAIR

This frozen fortress is where the Ice King lives. It's full of crazy caverns and dungeons. Princesses:

Stay away!

What do you think the different rooms in the Ice King's castle look like?

PRINCESS CAGE

KITCHEN/DINING ROOM

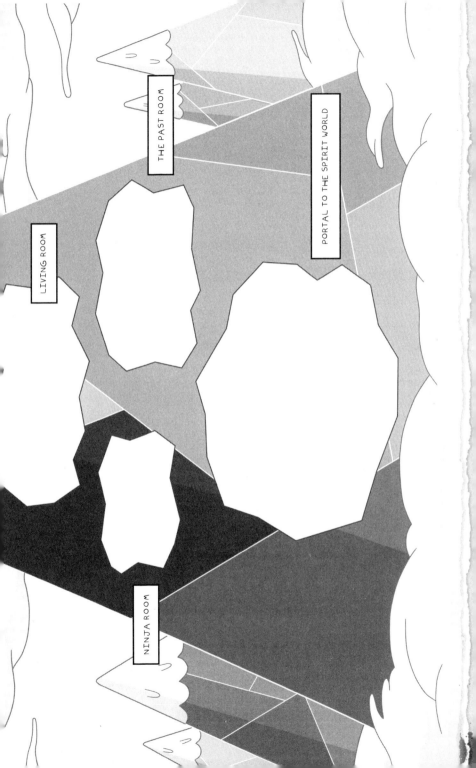

The Ice King's crown has cursed him with "wizard eyes." He sees crazy monsters and spirits that aren't really there.

Luckily, *you* don't have stanky old wizard eyes. But what if you did? Fill the scene below with imaginary monsters and spirits . . . and maybe a few princesses!

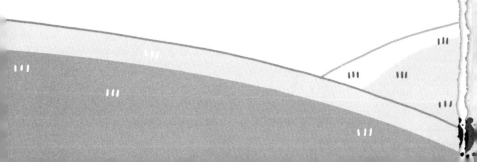

The Ice King has a supersad and tragic past.
Before he was a princess-chasing villain,
he was a nice dude named Simon Petrikov.
After the Mushroom War, he wandered a
postapocalyptic wasteland with young Marceline.

What would you do if the world ended tomorrow?

_____

_____

_____

What kind of monsters do you think would appear?

_____

_____

_____

Where would you and your friends hang out?

_____

_____

_____

Do you think there would be zombies?

_____

_____

_____

What if you ran into the Ice King? What would you do?

_____

_____

_____

_____

_____

_____

What do you think your hometown would look like after a mushroom war? Draw it below.

Ricardio the Heart Guy is the Ice King's heart, come to life! He tried to woo Princess Bubblegum because he wanted to "CUT OUT HER HEART AND MAKE OUT WITH IT!" That's what he said! His words! Creepy!

Write down ten really creepy sentences of your own—so you know what *not* to say to princesses.

That's not all I was going to do!

One time, the Ice King created his own princess by stealing parts from other princesses' bodies! From the different parts, he constructed **Princess Monster Wife.**

I'm just a bunch of stolen parts. I feel like a freak.

Best-Buddies Monster!

Grab bits and pieces and stuff from your friends, and create a monster! Try taking a lock of hair from one friend, a shoelace from your dad's shoe, some chewed-up bubblegum from your sister, and some fur from your dog. Use whatever you want!

Grab some tape and use the space below to create a horrible, disgusting, and terrifying Best-Buddies Monster!

Write a fresh song, and you'll be crushing it nonstop with the princesses.

The Ice King wrote a killer song by looking through his scrapbook for lyrical inspiration. You need to do the same!

Go through your house and find some junk from when you were just a baby, 'cause princesses love babies! Look for newspaper clippings, photos, letters—anything you can use to inspire you.

Tape that junk to the following pages, and write down how it makes you feel.

- SONG TIME -

Now go through all your photos, memories, and scrappy stuff, and write *one hot song!*

It's time for *you* to become a superpowerful, awesomely magical, princess-grabbing king or queen. Cut out a photo of yourself and tape it here. Or draw someone totally new! Up to you. No rules, yo.

NAME _____

What magic powers do you have? Circle some below, or write down new ones!

Control Minds

Flight

Magic Tail

Crazy Elastic

Change Sizes

Superpowered-Kick Feet

Superspeed

Control Fire

Control Ice

Control Electricity

Ridic Jumping Ability

Control Wind

Control Metal

Control Earth

Laser-Beam Fingertips

Shape-Shifting

Turbo Stink Breath

Unstoppable Dancing Power

Unbreakable Bones

The Ice King gets his ice powers from his magic crown. Now that you're a magic king or queen, do you have any magic clothing or armor? Write about it below, or draw it!

Do you have any pets, like Gunter? Or a magic sidekick, like Jake?

Create a pet or sidekick and draw it below. Be sure to give the dude a radical name.

_____
_____
_____
_____
_____
_____
_____
_____
_____
_____
_____
_____

_____'S
EVIL LAIR

Next, you need an evil lair, like the Ice King's. Will it be a castle on a cloud? Or an underground fortress? It can be whatever you want! Draw it here and label the most important rooms.

Finally, draw yourself in the middle of an epic battle with that other crazy villain—the Ice King!

Princess Bubblegum almost died after tangling with the evil Lich—and the Ice King was *not* happy about it. Ice King said that if PB died, he'd be "lost in his own labyrinth of emotions." Can you navigate the Ice King's labyrinth of emotions?

START

END

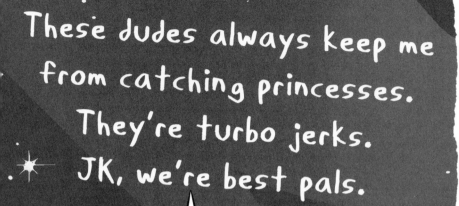

These dudes always keep me from catching princesses. They're turbo jerks. JK, we're best pals.

Why are we stuck inside the Ice King's book?

Yeah, we should be inside a *How to Kick a Bad Dude in the Butt* book!

Finn and Jake are best friends.

How much do you know about your best friend? Let's find out . . . Answer the questions below. When you're done, show the page to your friend and see how you did!

What is your best friend's . . .

Middle name?_____

Favorite movie?_____

Favorite video game?_____

Favorite food?_____

Favorite TV show?_____

Finn
likes Flame
Princess.

Hey!
Don't tell
everyone about
me and FP!

I slow dance all the time. With Gunter. For practice.

Has your best friend ever . . .

Skipped school? Yes / No

Slow danced? Yes / No

Broken an arm? Yes / No

Tooted in class? Yes / No

Does your best friend prefer . . .

Climbing trees or swimming?_____

Hamburgers or hot dogs?_____

Dance parties or freeze tag?_____

Ice-cream cones or sundaes?_____

Princess Bubblegum or Flame Princess?_____

43

Jake has kids now, which is weird—'cause sometimes parents are the worst, but Jake is pretty much the best.

I'm not gonna let anything happen to them!

PUPPIES!

If you had kids, what type of parent would you be?

What special rules would you have?

What do your parents do that you would definitely *not* do?

Why?

What if BMO were royalty? In what type of castle would majestic BMO live?

Draw it here!

I'm royal like frilly gold pants.

Lady Rainicorn is Jake's special lady friend. She's half rainbow and half unicorn. Totes weird.

Create your own "half one thing, half something else." Pick one word from each column below, then draw the crazy combo creation!

COLUMN 1:

Lightning
Tree
Boulder
Sand
Flower

COLUMN 2:

Goblin
Fairy
T. rex
Yeti
Dragon

SHHH!

I'M NOT TALKING TODAY

Finn and Jake once tried to go an entire day without talking. They used signs to communicate.

Keep track of how long you can go without talking! Total minutes without talking: _____

If you could only communicate using signs like Finn and Jake did, what ten signs would you definitely want to have?

ME NEITHER

If you need to tell someone something, write it here. You can write stuff like "Yo, I'm starvin'! Feed me, Ma!" or "Bring me more princesses to hang with!"

Finn thought he wasn't smart enough to impress a crowd of supersmart science dudes, so he acquired the magical Glasses of Nerdicon. The magic specs made him supersmart—but also caused a disaster to go down.

Is there something you'd like to change about yourself? What would happen if you could change it?

Everything smallish is just a small version of something big!!!! I understand everything!!!!

Are there any magical items,
like glasses, that you would use
to make this change? Draw them!

Describe your normal morning. Do you walk to school? Do you get a ride? Do you take the bus?

Now, imagine you're suddenly transported into the Land of Ooo! What happens next?

Do you run into any pretty princesses on your adventure? How does your adventure end?

Marceline once told Finn that what girls really like is excitement. So if you want to catch a princess, you have to be an exciting, adventurous dude like Finn!

This is *your* adventure page, where you prove you're an adventurer! Here's how:

Wear the same pair of pants *all weekend*—and don't empty your pockets until the weekend is over!

What do you find when you empty them? Everything inside is evidence of your adventure!

The more pocket junk, the better the adventure! Bonus points for dead bugs.

Tape your pocket junk to these pages.

Did you have an adventuresome weekend?
Adventurous enough to make a cute princess smile?

One time, the Ice King froze PB and she shattered into a bunch of pieces. The doctors were able to reassemble her—sorta . . . They brought her back as a thirteen-year-old instead of an eighteen-year-old! When she woke up, she was five years younger!

What were you like five years ago?

_____

_____

_____

_____

What do you think your life will be like five years from now? Why?

_____

_____

_____

_____

_____

_____

_____

PB created the
"most perfect sandwich"
that ever existed.

PB FACT!
She loves
spaghetti.

What's the most perfect food you've ever eaten?

If you could eat one food every day for the rest of your life,
what would it be?

What's better—chocolate, vanilla, or pepperoni?

Nachos—good or bad?

Describe the worst meal you've ever eaten.

What if you could create the most perfect food that ever existed? Would it be pizza with ice cream on top? Chicken fingers coated in marshmallow? Salsa hot dogs? Would you serve it to your special princess?

Draw *your* most perfect food ever below, and give it a delicious name.

The Lich is crazy evil and has crazy evil powers—including mind control! One time he entered Princess Bubblegum's mind, and all sorts of bad junk went down.

If you could control other people's minds, what would you do? Would you make your teacher do somersaults? Or make your parents give you the keys to their car?

Write your ultimate mind-control fantasy below.

If I could control princesses' minds, I'd make them come over and give me hugs.

61

If you want to win PB's heart, you need to battle some candy zombies with her—like Finn did!

Do you have a candy-zombie-fighting plan?

If candy zombies took over the world, what would you do?

What type of weapon would you use to fight a colossal army of candy zombies?

Draw the most *terrifying*, *ferocious*, and *buttery* candy zombie you can imagine.

Want a surefire way to catch a princess? Win a wizard battle! Whichever wizard wins a wizard battle gets a smooch from Princess Bubblegum.

HOT STUFF!

Draw the most furiously fantastic wizard battle ever!
Stuff the scene full of wizards and witches!
Draw yourself in there, too, if you want!

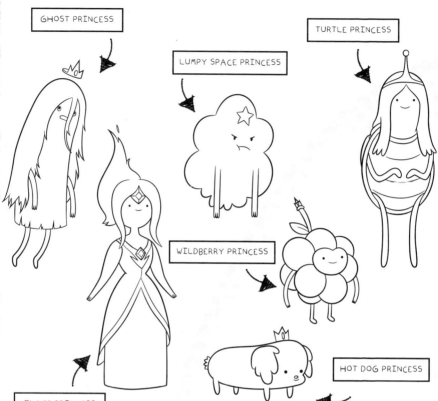

GHOST PRINCESS

TURTLE PRINCESS

LUMPY SPACE PRINCESS

WILDBERRY PRINCESS

FLAME PRINCESS

HOT DOG PRINCESS

There are a TON
of princesses in the
Land of Ooo.
These are some of the
Ice King's favorites.

Wildberry Princess rules the Wildberry Kingdom.
At the center of the kingdom is this huge, radical bush.
Draw some other Wildberry creatures doing fun Wildberry stuff.

SAP HAPPY

Flame Princess was once Finn's girlfriend. When Finn wanted to write her a sappy poem, he watched the sunrise to get inspiration.

But you don't need to watch the sunrise—you just need to look at something that inspires you! Trees, a video-game cover, some old socks . . . whatever gets your juices flowing! **Now write a supersappy haiku!**

A haiku is a three-line poem that *doesn't rhyme.* The first line has five syllables, the second line has seven syllables, and the third line has five syllables. Like this:

Line #1: Five syllables

_____

_____

_____

Line #2: Seven syllables

_____

_____

_____

Line #3: Five syllables

_____

_____

When Finn and Jake made their own movie, they put Slime Princess in it. Now it's time to cast Slime Princess as the hero in *your* movie!

What's the title of your slimy movie?

What type of character does Slime Princess play? Is she a spy? A dragon hunter? A slime ninja?!

The Ice King is totally the bad guy, right? So . . . what's the Ice King's villainous plot?

You're gonna make me a star!

Draw an eye-catching poster for your movie.

In the Land of Ooo, there are a bunch of food princesses that rule over food kingdoms. There's Hot Dog Princess, Breakfast Princess, Toast Princess—there's a whole grocery store full of 'em!

Turn your favorite food into a princess and draw her below.

I'D EAT THEM ALL!

Finn and Flame Princess went on a dungeon-crawl date—and fought all sorts of funky monsters down there. Dungeon exploring is serious business . . .

Write down ten places you'd like to explore.

We can check this one off our list!

There are a whole buttload of awesome princesses in the Land of Ooo. Now it's time to stretch your imagination to the limit and create your own princess!

Name: _____

Kingdom: _____

_____

Is your princess supersmart? Way immature? Athletically awesome? Describe her here:

_____

_____

_____

_____

_____

_____

_____

_____

_____

Draw your princess here!

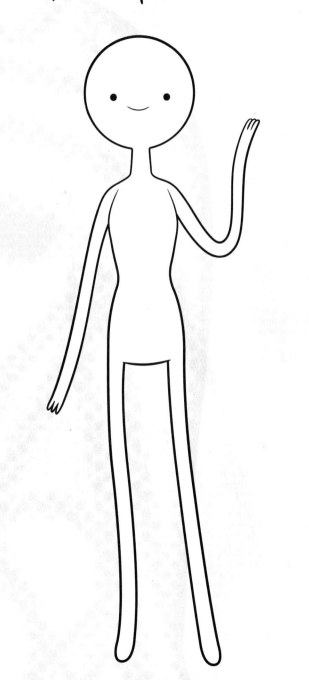

Now, draw your princess's kingdom.
Need inspiration? Maybe it's underwater.
Or upside down? Or made of cheese? Or
made of hoodies?

LSP is always getting into major fights with her lumpy parents.

Write ten things about *your* parents that drive you nuts.
But that's not all! Write five things about your parents that you actually really love. Because they can't be all bad!

My parents are
horrible idiots.
I LUMPING
HATE THEM!

QUIZ TIME!

Which Is the Right Princess for You?

Circle your answers, and LSP will determine the right princess for you!

1) Which type of adventure are you most likely to get into?
- A. Chasing an escaped science-experiment monster
- B. Exploring a dungeon
- C. Any adventure in which you get to destroy stuff
- D. A totally lumpy adventure

2) It's your first date! You:
- A. Head straight to Make-Out Point
- B. Sneak around and scare dudes
- C. Fight candy zombies
- D. Share poetry

I'll totes help you find the perfect princess! I'm a lumping fab matchmaker. Let's take this quiz!

3) It's a super rainy, lousy day. You:
- A. Huddle up under some trees and suck on beans
- B. Watch a movie with your friends
- C. Stay inside— you hate getting wet!
- D. Rock out like a rock star

4) You'd be happiest if someone described you as:
- A. Totes outrageous
- B. Not evil
- C. Mischievous
- D. Responsible

5) You decide to have a quiet night inside. For dinner, you want:

A. Something red! Whatever it is—just make it red!
B. Everything Burrito
C. Piping-hot soup
D. Candy, candy, candy

6) How would you describe yourself?

A. Smart—supersmart—and responsible!
B. Laid-back, chill, and a little goth
C. Totes full of drama!
D. Caring and patient

Now use the key below to add up your points. For example, if you answered B for question #1, that's 2 points!

Question 1: A = 1 point, B = 2 points, C = 3 points, D = 4 points
Question 2: A = 4 points, B = 2 points, C = 1 point, D = 4 points
Question 3: A = 4 points, B = 1 point, C = 3 points, D = 2 points
Question 4: A = 4 points, B = 3 points, C = 2 points, D = 1 point
Question 5: A = 2 points, B = 4 points, C = 3 points, D = 1 point
Question 6: A = 1 point, B = 2 points, C = 4 points, D = 3 points

Now let's find out which princess is right for you. If you scored . . .

8 points or fewer: Love! Your perfect princess is PB!

9-13 points: Ooh. You're a dark soul. You'd match up well with Marceline.

14-19 points: Is there evil in your blood? You and Flame Princess would be one hot item.

20 + points: Oh my lumping glob! You and LSP were, like, made for each other.

ON YOUR OWN

Can you imagine living *totally* alone?
Do you think you'd like it?

_____

_____

_____

_____

Where would you choose to live?
Would you live by a campfire, like LSP?

_____

_____

_____

_____

What would be the scariest part of living totally alone?

_____

_____

_____

_____

_____

One time I ran away from my parents house 'cause they're the worst. I lived in a hobo camp and ate beans. It was ah-mazing.

List five things you'd definitely bring with you.

I feel like the Ice King is getting a bad rap in this book. He isn't all bad. He's just been warped by his wizardness.
Aww, thanks, Marceline.

Marceline always wears rad T-shirts.

Design your own T-shirt—one you think Marceline would be proud to wear.

It's good practice—you gotta be stylish to catch a princess! That's why I wear this fashion-forward blue robe.

Marceline once sang a killer song about her real-deal feelings. Sometimes songs are good for junk like that.

Use the next two pages to write a song and spill your funky, sensitive guts! If it's too personal, just rip it out and tear it up when you're done.

A PRINCESS AND A QUEEN!

Write and draw your own comic starring two of the baddest girls in the Land of Ooo.

BUT WHO WOULD HAVE SUSPECTED . . . ?

AT LAST . . .

THE END!

Marceline has been alive for a long time. A way long time. That's because she's a vampire and she's immortal.

Would you like to be immortal?

_____

_____

What do you think the world will be like in ten years?

_____

_____

What do you think the world will be like in one thousand years?

_____

_____

What are five memories you would never forget, no matter how old you got?

_____

_____

TIME CAPSULE

Marceline knows all about how weird it is to live forever. She's got megaloads of memories! So here's a Marceline-style challenge ... In the space below, write about your day today.

Today's date: _____

What did you wear? _____

_____

What did you do? _____

_____

_____

_____

Did anything great happen? Or did something terrible happen?
Did you meet any princesses?

_____

_____

_____

_____

_____

_____

_____

Now, turn the page ...

Now tear this page out of the journal! Fold it up, tiny and small, and hide it.

One year from today, go find your torn-out page, unfold it, read it, and answer the questions below:

What has changed since last year?

_____

_____

_____

Do you seem older?

_____

_____

_____

Are you still as awesome as you were one year ago?

_____

_____

_____

Have you caught a princess yet?!

_____

_____

_____

Marceline is a vampire queen— but where is her vampire king?!

Draw a radical vampire king for Marceline to get cuddly with.

Don't make him too, y'know— like Finn!

What Time Is It?

Turn back to pages 30 and 76. Write a story about your king or queen trying to catch your princess!

Make sure the Ice King gets involved to junk things up, Ice King-style.

STORY TIME!

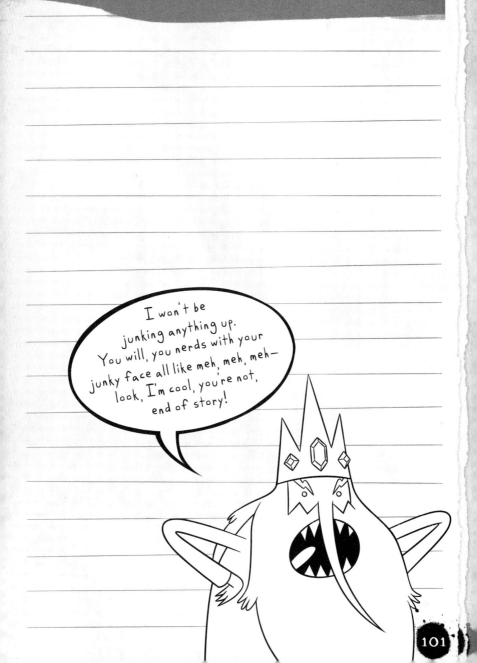

I won't be junking anything up. You will, you nerds with your junky face all like meh, meh, meh— look, I'm cool, you're not, end of story!